Geese Police on Patrol

Lynda Bulla

Cover Art by Cindy Prieto
Chapter Art by Franco Costales

Halo
PUBLISHING
INTERNATIONAL

ISBN: 978-1-61244-965-4
LCCN: 2021903754

Halo Publishing International, LLC
8000 W Interstate 10, Suite 600
San Antonio, Texas 78230
www.halopublishing.com

Printed and bound in the United States of America

To my great-grandchildren: Follow your passion
wherever it leads you. This one is for you.

Contents

Geese Police on Patrol

Chapter One

The Case of the Missing Egg

"*Cluck,* help! I've been robbed," Rumples squawked. "Help, police."

"Geese Police at your service! What happened?" Sergeant Gander asked as he ran up next to the chicken coop.

"I was out hunting bugs and grubs, and when I went back to my nest, one egg was gone."

Officer Drake arrived and asked, "Who else in the coop when you left?"

"Rhody was there on her nest."

Her friends gathered around to hear what the excitement was all about.

Sergeant Gander asked the gathered fowl, "Anyone know anything about this crime?"

"*Cluck*, NO!" they all answered excitedly.

"Oh my," Henrietta squawked. "A thief in the henhouse! Oh my, oh my!" she squawked again, flapping her wings.

Andy ran squawking, "This is just awful. How are we ever to feel safe again? Stolen eggs. What next?"

Sergeant Gander stood calmly in the middle of the yard. "Settle down, ladies. We have it firmly under control. No one is in any danger. I'm sure we will find the culprit."

Officer Drake went into the coop and found Rhody asleep on her nest. "Rhody."

"*Cluck*, huh?" Rhody blinked as she woke up.

"Did you see anyone take Rumples's egg?"

"*Cluck!* No!" She sat up with a start at Officer Drake's question. "What happened?" She carefully stood and got off her nest.

The officer noted a clue; four light-brown eggs were nestled in the straw. "Rumples says someone took an egg from her nest while she was gone. Are those all yours?"

"*Cluck*, yes! My eggs are brown; hers are cream colored," Rhody said. "Officer Drake, I hope you find who did it. We can't have our eggs go missing. That's just not right." Rhody carefully settled herself back on her nest.

Meanwhile, Sergeant Gander checked the outside of the coop for clues. Following slithery lines in the dirt, Sergeant Gander went to a small hole in the ground. "Gar, are you home?"

The brown-striped garter snake poked his head up, his slender tongue darting quickly in and out, tasting the air to discover who had interrupted his nap.

"SSSSSSSSSSSSure, I'm here. What do you want Sergeant Gander?" he hissed.

"Someone stole one of Rumples's eggs. What did you have for breakfast?"

"A nice fat frog!" he said, retreating back into his den underground.

"Prove it," Sergeant Gander challenged.

Gar stretched out, revealing the outline of a frog about midway down his otherwise slender form. "Now, go away and let me finisssh my nap. You're giving me an upssset sssssssssssstomach. I must let this frog digesssssssssssssst."

He followed some small, flat prints. "Skeet, are you here?"

Skeet, a brown lizard, could blend in with almost anything. "I'm right here, Sergeant. What's all the fuss about?"

"Someone stole an egg from Rumples's nest. I don't suppose you know anything about it?"

"Me, eat a chicken egg? As if that's even possible. I will keep my ears open and let you know if I hear anything."

Officer Drake, on the other side of the yard, found small prints, barely noticeable in the dirt, that led him to a large crack on the side of the coop. Cream-colored eggshell pieces were scattered around. Recognizing the prints, the officer yelled. "Sly. Where's Sly?"

Sly, the rat, was hiding in a pile of leaves near the fence line. He rustled the leaves upon hearing his name.

Officer Drake turned toward the noise and spotted the rat. He hurried towards him.

Sly ran!

Sergeant Gander also took off after the runaway rat. Both geese caught up to Sly as he was about to squeeze through a hole in the fence. Sergeant Gander picked him up by his tail.

Sly twisted and wiggled, trying to get out of the tight hold. "Ouch. Let me go. Ouch. That hurts," Sly whined.

"Good," Officer Drake honked. "Nothing you don't deserve. Shame on you, stealing Rumples's egg. There are plenty of things to eat around here. You don't have to steal."

"It just looked so tempting. I couldn't help myself. I promise not to do it again," Sly said.

"I've heard that before. Tell it to the judge," Officer Drake replied.

Sergeant Gander kept a firm grip on Sly until he was safely inside the cell at headquarters. "You can't be eating the hens' eggs," Gander honked. "Get comfortable, you're going to be here for a while. Judge Hoot won't be back for a week."

Sly stretched out on the bunk and muttered, "I guess my momma was right. Crime doesn't pay."

"Officer Drake, thank you for catching that mean old rat," squawked Rumples. "We're so lucky you're here, keeping this barnyard safe."

"The Geese Police are on patrol and happy to be of service," he honked. He turned to Sergeant Gander. "Crime solved, case closed, and peace is restored. Those ladies can sure put up a squawk when they're unhappy. I hope nothing else ruffles their feathers."

Sergeant Gander nodded. "Me too!"

16

Chapter Two

Cygnet Trouble

It was a peaceful day at the pond. Buccinator and Molly took turns dipping under the water to eat the tender roots from the lush water plants. Molly kept a watchful eye on their five curious cygnets while Buccinator scanned the sky for danger.

"*HONK!!*" Buccinator called out a loud warning when he saw a scary, red cloud with a long tail, floating towards them.

Molly anxiously called her hatchlings to her side as she watched the strange object come closer. They all swam to her, except Sissy, who was busy examining a beetle.

The object landed right next to Sissy. Molly honked, "Sissy, be careful!"

"Oh, Mom, I'm okay." Sissy approached the object, pecking at it. It floated in the water near her. She felt something wrap around her legs. She had trouble paddling. "Mom, help! I'm caught!"

Molly flew over with Buccinator right behind. Buccinator dipped his head into the water to see what happened. The water was cloudy and dark.

"Let's push her to shore," said Molly.

On a flat rock hidden in the reeds, Gar, the garter snake, watched.

When Molly and Buccinator got Sissy to shore, she was so tangled she couldn't stand. She lay at the water's edge, trembling with fear. "Mom, help me!" she pleaded.

Gar slithered to the shore. "What'ssss the trouble?" he hissed. His forked tongue darted in and out, trying to discover the problem. Buccinator pecked at Gar to chase him off.

Gar slithered through the reeds and headed to the barnyard for help.

Officer Drake guarded the gate as Gar slithered up. "Sssssissy'sss in trouble at the pond," he hissed. "I tried to help but Buccinator attacked me."

Officer Drake honked across the yard to get Sergeant Gander's attention. "Trouble with the swans; let's go take a look," he said. "Thanks, Gar, I'll let them know you came for help."

Officer Drake flew low over the reeds and landed near Sissy, her eyes wide with fear. Sergeant Gander also arrived and assessed the situation. "Unidentified object wrapped around the cygnet," he said, taking notes for his incident report.

Sissy wiggled and squirmed, further entangling herself. "Mommy, Mommy. Help me," Sissy cried.

Molly honked sorrowfully. "Oh, Sissy. I'm sure you'll be just fine. Let the nice policemen do their job. Just lie still. Don't get tangled any worse than you are. Please, baby, be still. Shhh. It's going to be fine," she crooned softly.

Sly, the rat, peeked from the reeds. "Hey, can I help?"

"No!" said Molly and Buccinator. "Get out of here!"

"Let's see if we can untangle her," Sergeant Gander said. "Back up, everyone, give us some room."

Molly took several steps back, but Buccinator stood his ground, flapped his wings, and squawked loudly.

Officer Drake tried to calm him. "Buccinator! If you want us to help, you have to get out of the way."

Sergeant Gander rolled the small swan, over and over, trying to unwind the string. It was no use. The string had tied itself into several knots.

"You sure I can't help?" said Sly from behind the reeds.

Sergeant Gander ignored him and said, "Molly, try and peck through the string."

She tried. "OW!" Sissy said.

"It's wrapped too tight!" Molly said.

"What are we going to do?" Buccinator said, pacing.

Once more, Sly said, "Let me help."

"Stay away from my baby, you egg-stealing beast," Molly snapped.

"Wait!" said Officer Drake. "Maybe he can help. Sly, can you gnaw through this thing without hurting Sissy? You have the sharpest teeth of all."

"I'll try," he said. "Just keep Buccinator away from me."

"He won't hurt you. I am right here. But don't hurt Sissy, or you'll answer to all of us," said Officer Drake.

Sly carefully approached the baby. "If you want my help, you have to hold real still."

Sissy froze! Those big rat teeth were very scary.

Sly grabbed a piece of the string with his front paw, pulled it gently to his mouth and started chewing. He had it apart in no time and began on the next piece. A small cheer went up each time he chewed through a piece of it.

Soon, the small swan was free. She rolled over and stood up, fluffing her tiny wings. Molly drew her close, wrapping her big wings around her cygnet. She loaded her babies onto her back and slid gracefully into the water.

Buccinator approached Sly and quietly said, "Thanks, Sly. We owe you an apology."

Officer Drake said, "You owe Gar one too. He came for help. Glad we could all work together to solve the problem. And tell your young'uns to stay away from things that don't belong in the pond. That stuff is a danger to us all. Floats in, pollutes the pond, tangles up baby swans. There is just no end to the trouble those things cause."

"Oh, thank you. You two are heroes everyday," Molly honked elatedly.

Buccinator wiped at his eye with his wing. "Thank you. You saved our baby. We're so grateful."

"You're welcome, Buccinator. Better have the eye checked. You keep wiping it with your wing," Officer Drake honked in amusement. He was glad there weren't any serious injuries.

"The Geese Police are on patrol and happy to be of service," they said as they flew low over the pond and back to the barnyard.

Chapter Three

The Case of
the Disappearing Water

"Sergeant Gander, come quick. You're needed at the pond. The water's gone." Skeet, the lizard, darted this way and that.

"What do you mean, gone?" the sergeant asked.

"It's a mystery. Hurry! You have to see this for yourself. It's the strangest thing. Water doesn't just disappear. It comes in one end of the pond and goes out the other. It's going out, but not coming in."

"We'll check it out," Sergeant said.

Sergeant Gander called Officer Drake, and off they flew to the pond.

Grandfather Bullfrog sat on a rock that was almost completely out of the water. "*Croak.* Help. It's all mud. Ick. I can't leave this rock. I don't want to get my lovely yellow, spotted waistcoat dirty. You're the authority around here. What's going on? Where has the water gone? This just isn't acceptable. *Croak.*" Grandfather Bullfrog's great googly eyes bulged with irritation.

Officer Drake looked around in horror. Small fish flopped around in shrinking pools of water. The tall reeds usually had their feet in the shallow water along the edge, but now stood high and dry.

Buccinator and Molly and their half-grown cygnets huddled together on one side of the pond. Their heads were bent, and their rounded beaks nearly touched the ground. "Our beautiful pond! It's gone! Ruined! What are you going to do about it, Sergeant?" Buccinator said with a mournful honk.

"We're going to get to the bottom of this! Hopefully, before all the water is completely gone," Sergeant Gander answered.

"Come on, Officer Drake. Let's fly upstream and see what's going on."

The two geese took off, gaining altitude so they could get a good view of the area. About a mile upstream from the pond, they located the problem—a large structure built almost entirely across the narrow stream.

"Let's go find out who built this dam," Sergeant said.

Landing gracefully on the edge of the stream, they shouted, "Hello, is anyone home?"

The dam, constructed of twigs and mud, appeared quite large. A strange-looking animal came waddling around from the side. "Who wants to know?" he replied rather gruffly.

"Excuse me, sir," Officer Drake continued. "We come from the pond about a mile downstream. We noticed your creation is stopping the water. My name is Officer Drake and this is Sergeant Gander. We're the Geese Police on patrol in this area. May I ask your name?"

"I'm Marlo the Muskrat. Not that it's any of your business. I built my home here, and here I'll stay. Had to move once, not doin' it again."

"But, Marlo, you've blocked the whole stream and water can't pass through."

"So."

"Fish are dying; Grandfather Bullfrog is high and dry atop a rock in the middle of what used to be a lovely pond. The swans and their babies are hiding in the reeds, trying to figure out what happened. Where are you from and how did you come to be here?" Sergeant Gander said pleasantly.

"I came here 'cause I didn't think I'd be bothered. Don't much like being bothered," Marlo responded.

"We're truly sorry to bother you. You did a super job with your dam-building skills. Anyone would think you were a beaver. But if we could find a way to get some water downstream, it would help our friends," Officer Drake responded.

"Dam? It's not a dam. It's my house. Don't like beavers. Never did. They have those ugly flat tails that go splat in the water. Make a big splash, they do. Scare the fish. 'Tis why I moved here. Beavers came and chased me out. 'Twas a lot of work building my new home. But now it's all flooded inside. I was trying to figure out what to do when you two came honking your way onto my property," Marlo said.

"Let me get this straight—you built your house and it wasn't flooded, but now it is? Does that about sum it up?" Sergeant asked.

"Yup. My bedroom is totally underwater. I don't sleep underwater. I just use the water to keep out creatures that want to eat me. You know, like wolves and badgers and the like. But my bed should be dry. Any suggestions?"

"As a matter of fact, I do," said Officer Drake. "Your house has created a dam across the stream. The water coming in from upstream has nowhere to go. It just keeps rising and getting deeper. If we redesign your home just a bit, letting some water out to flow downstream, I think we can solve all the problems."

"Don't you go messing with my house. Just tell me what to do, and I'll do it!" Marlo snorted.

"Take a little off the structure on this side and add it on over around the edge of the bank. It will allow the water to flow out. You sure you don't want our help?" asked Officer Drake.

"Nah, I'll do it. Let's see if your bright idea has any merit," he responded.

Marlo got busy moving twigs and mud. He took from one side and built up the other, just as Officer Drake suggested. Soon a tiny rivulet of water started to flow downstream. By the time Marlo finished, the stream flowed almost as much as before.

"Thanks for your help, Marlo. It was nice meeting you," the Geese Police said as they prepared to return to the pond. "If you ever need us, let us know."

"Yeah, yeah. Thanks for solving my problem, but I'd be happiest if you just left me alone." With that, Marlo dove under the water and into his newly designed home.

Arriving back at the pond, the Geese Police found Grandfather Bullfrog still atop the rock. With a bellowing croak, he thanked the Geese Police for a job well done. The swans paddled around the pond once more with all their cygnets. Life was back to normal.

As Sergeant Gander and Officer Drake returned to the barnyard, they reviewed the day's events. "He was a crusty cayote," said Officer Drake.

"But he worked with us and got the job done," agreed Sergeant Gander.

"You never know what each day will bring," the young officer said.

"And this one was no exception," finished Sergeant Gander as he closed the file.

Chapter Four

The Guinea Fowl Gang

"Officer Drake, those guinea fowl are bullies. They pulled out my lovely tail feathers. Then they chased me out of the coop. They are mean, noisy ruffians." Rhody fluffed her feathers in agitation, indignant with such treatment.

Henrietta and Andy gathered around the injured hen and *cluck*ed in sympathy. "Oh, your gorgeous tail feathers, gone. Oh my, oh my," they all exclaimed. "That gang has got to go."

Sergeant Gander strode into the yard. "What have they done this time?" he asked.

Ever since the guinea fowl had arrived in the barnyard, things were not the same. The small chicks had grown into rambunctious keets. Now they were a gang of noisy, troublesome youngsters. They resembled rugby footballs, and where one went, they all went. The twenty-five or so guinea fowl were all colors. There were whites, royal purples, pearls, and lavenders. Grotesque wattles popped out of their heads, above and below their orange beaks. The flock seemed to have no idea what was happening, except to eat, sleep, chatter, and scream in terror. They constantly looked for ways to stir up trouble.

In the coop, the male guinea fowl would harass the roosters, keeping them away from the food, water, and sleep. They ran them ragged. During the day, they perched in trees and on fences. Being good flyers, they wandered away regularly. Many of the other inhabitants of the barnyard wished them gone for good.

Sergeant Gander waddled over to where the guinea fowl had gathered. They were huddled around a wooden stick on the ground.

"What's that?"

"I don't know."

"What's what?"

"That!"

"What's that?"

"You okay?"

"I'm okay."

"Good over here."

"Wait, what was that?"

"Oh goodness, oh goodness, oh goodness."

"Look out. Look out!"

"Run, run!"

And they started to scatter as they screamed and screeched.

"Hold it," Sergeant Gander honked in his most official voice.

The flock stopped, forgetting what terrifying event had set them off.

"Hi, Sergeant," they said in unison. "What's up?"

"I'm not telling you again; leave the chickens alone."

"What are you talking about? We didn't do anything to the chickens. We've been here all afternoon, making sure this snake doesn't attack us."

"That's a stick, not a snake," Officer Drake said as he joined the crowd.

"Oh yeah. I knew that," said Puchie, the apparent leader of the gang. "I just wanted to see if anyone else knew it too." Puchie waved his colorful crest around, trying to appear important.

"Well, that's not what this is about. Leave the chickens alone. No more stealing their food, pulling out their tail feathers, and harassing the roosters. You're going to be fox food outside of the coop if you keep causing trouble."

"We didn't do nothin', Officer," said Numda. He was a helmeted guinea fowl and looked a bit like a military helmet with legs.

Egelli, the black guinea hen, let out another screech, stampeding the flock once again. "A dog, I saw a dog. Run, run."

"That isn't a dog. It's a tree stump. You're the goofiest bunch of fowl I've ever known," Officer Drake exclaimed. "Focus on the problem. No more trouble with the chickens."

"Yeah, yeah, we know," said Edourdi, his crested top just beginning to grow some lovely plumage.

"What was he talking about?" said Guttera.

"I have no idea, something about the chickens," screeched Puchie.

"Speaking of chickens, let's go find some lunch," said Numda.

Clouds gathered and the wind started to blow. All the chickens took shelter in the coop. The geese went back to the station house. The swan family found some tall reeds to nest in. Gar, the garter snake, burrowed into his den, and Sly, the rat, hid under the corncrib. A big storm was coming.

The guinea fowl didn't pay attention to the approaching storm. They kept chattering and screeching among themselves. A few flew up into the trees that surrounded the barnyard, but most stayed on the ground, hunting for stray kernels of corn.

A big, twisting wind roared. It sounded like a train coming straight at the barnyard. The wind picked up the birds and tossed them high into the air. It scattered the flock of guinea fowl like bowling pins.

The wind swept away anything that wasn't tied down, cleaning the yard of all loose debris. When things got quiet again, the chickens began to venture out of the coop. The Geese Police wandered back to see if there was any damage. For a while, no one noticed that the guinea fowl were missing.

Sly, the rat, said it first, "Where are those noisy, crazy birds?"

Officer Drake looked around, suddenly aware of the extreme quiet of the barnyard. No guinea fowl anywhere.

"We need to organize a search party and find out what has become of them," he said to Sergeant Gander.

"Who's going to go? No one here even liked them, and they picked on everybody," Officer Drake asked.

"It's still our job to round them up and bring them back. Protect and serve, remember?"

They asked for help from the sparrows in the field, the horses that roamed in the next pasture, and even Gar helped spread the word. Days went by with no sign of the crazy gang of birds.

Almost a week later, the sound of screeching and arguing could be heard coming through the tall grass in the pasture.

"I told you it was here."

"What was here?"

"Home!"

"Are we there yet?"

"Yes."

And a slightly smaller band of guinea fowl fluttered pell-mell into the barnyard. They looked tired and beaten up. They were also glad to be home.

"Welcome back, Numda!" said Officer Drake. "Where have you been? We've been looking all over for you."

"The wind blew us far, far away. And we argued our way back home."

"Don't be so foolish the next time the wind blows. Take some shelter. But don't pick on the chickens."

At that moment, Gar slithered his way into the yard. "Hey, they got back. Welcome home."

"Oh my. A snake, a snake, run, run, run."

"A SNAKE!!!!" they all cried in unison.

Sergeant Gander smiled as Gar sighed. "It's nice to know some things don't change."

Chapter Five

The Case of the Fainting Goat

"Yo, Officer Drake. There's a problem in the meadow," Skeet, the lizard, called breathlessly from atop the fence post that surrounded the barnyard.

"What happened? Did someone get hurt?" Officer Drake replied.

"I don't know. Beetal asked me to come get you, and here I am," Skeet said.

"Sergeant, hurry, we need to go check on the goats," Officer Drake honked.

The two Geese Police flew over the fence and into the meadow beyond. They didn't know much about the new residents in the meadow. The herd of goats had arrived a week or so ago and were busy eating almost everything in sight. The meadow had lots of tall grass and weeds. Some of those weeds were poison oak. It was starting to take over, so the goats were brought in to eat it up. Poison oak is good for goats, and they thought it was delicious.

Beetal, a large brown goat with a nice beard, was the largest goat in the field. He had appointed himself as the leader of the herd.

Sergeant Gander spotted Beetal and the rest of the herd huddled around in a circle. Gander and Drake landed in the middle and saw a young white-and-brown goat lying stiff legged on its side.

Officer Drake could see the goat was breathing, but it appeared to be frozen in fear. "What happened here?" Officer Drake demanded.

"We don't know. Is he going to be all right?" said Beetal.

"Start at the beginning and tell us what happened. First off, do you know his name?"

Beetal replied, "I think his name is Myo. He is new to the herd. He just arrived this morning. We were all enjoying the lush grass and scrub brush. We worked our way around a tree trunk where lots of yummy poison oak grows. I introduced myself, barely got his name, and Skeet ran by and up the tree. All of a sudden, Myo went stiff as a board and fell over into a faint. I don't know how or why."

"Skeet? Are you around here?"

"Yo, Officer. I'm right here."

"Did you see or do anything to make Myo faint?" Officer Drake asked.

"No, man. I did not. I don't want to be responsible for this. I just go about my business, basking in the sun and eating insects. I don't hurt and don't want to be hurt. I came by to introduce myself to the new arrival. I mean, the goats always have their noses to the ground. You know, Officer, they are real eating machines. They cleared a whole patch of brush where I was hiding from a hawk. I just wanted to let the new one know I was sharing the meadow, so he wouldn't eat me while he was busy eating weeds. I do stay well hidden when I want to, you know," the striped, brown-and-grey lizard said as he puffed with pride.

"Thank you, Skeet," Officer Drake said and began to move around the herd, taking everyone's statement. They all told the same story—the lizard ran by and the goat fainted.

Sergeant Gander was standing guard over the little goat, making sure he was okay. It wasn't long before the goat blinked, twitched, stretched, baaed, and stood up, unconcerned and unaffected by his apparent problem.

"Myo, are you okay? Can you tell us what happened?" Sergeant Gander said in his most gentle voice. He didn't want to scare the young goat and perhaps cause him to faint again.

Myo looked around in wonder. All eyes were on him, waiting for an answer.

"Oh my, I'm so sorry I caused anyone to worry. I'm Myo, the fainting goat. My mom and dad were both very good at fainting, and it looks like I am too. We faint when we're happy or scared or for any reason at all. You see, I saw something run by. I thought it might be a snake. I'm afraid of snakes."

Skeet perched on a boulder and listened to Myo. He cleared his throat. "Yo, Myo, ahem, over here on the boulder. I'm sorry I scared you, but I'm no snake. I'm Skeet, a lizard. I eat insects, not goats. I share this meadow with you, and I was coming over to introduce myself when all this happened."

Myo looked a bit ashamed. "How do you do," he said. "I won't faint again when you run by. But who are you?" he said, turning toward the Geese Police.

"Officer Drake and Sergeant Gander at your service," Sergeant Gander replied. "We are the Geese Police on patrol. *Protect and serve* is our motto. Now we know that this could be a regular event with you, we'll try not to cause such a fuss. And just so you know, there is only one snake around here. His name is Gar, and he is a green garter snake. He is very nice and won't hurt you at all. Please try not to be afraid of him. I will let him know of your unusual problem and ask that he try to watch out for you. I am glad this case is solved."

Officer Drake and Sergeant Gander flew back to the barnyard, leaving the goats to their brush-clearing work. "A fainting goat! Now I've seen everything," Officer Drake remarked. "I wonder what could possibly be more unusual than that?"

Better
Hens
and Giblets

Chapter Six

Theodore's Lost Gobble

"*Chirrup, chirrup.* Oh, good morning...*chirrup*...Officer Drake. *Chirrup!*" said Theodore, the forlorn turkey.

"Goodness, Theodore. What's that dreadful noise you're making?"

"Officer Drake...*chirrup*...I have the...*chirrup*...hiccups. I can't gobble. *Chirrup!!*"

Theodore slumped on the ground, and his feathers ruffled with each hiccup.

"I can't gobble, walk, play, or eat. *Chirrup.* These hiccups... *chirrup*...are just awful. Do you know how to get rid of... *chirrup*...hiccups?" Theodore asked hopefully. "*Chirrup, chirrup, chirrup.*"

Officer Drake tried to keep from smiling at Theodore's dilemma, but the poor bird sounded so peculiar. "I'll ask the sergeant," he replied and quickly turned away to keep from laughing.

"Hiccups? Now I've heard everything!" said Sergeant Gander. "How DO we cure the hiccups?"

"Let me ask around and see what our barnyard family says about this," Officer Drake said.

"Rumples, do you know how to cure hiccups?" he asked.

Rumples, busy chasing down a particularly large grub, asked, "What? Huh? Hiccups? Who has the hiccups?"

"Theodore. He lost his gobble. He's making a most peculiar sound." Officer Drake laughed.

"Hiccups! Hmmmm! I've heard drinking water can cure hiccups."

Rumples gave up on the chase for the grub, and ran off to gather her friends and spread the news. A turkey with hiccups, one that can't gobble! Why that's almost as good as a goat that faints. There was nothing better for the hens than a juicy piece of gossip, unless it was a big, fat grub.

Soon the entire flock of chickens gathered around the poor turkey. *"Chirrup, chirrup, chirrup!"*

"Water. He needs to drink water."

"No, salt will do it."

"Water!"

"Salt!"

"Water!"

Rumples and Henrietta faced each other, each determined that their cure would save poor Theodore.

"Water is closer. Does he drink it or stick his head in it?" Rhody asked.

"Well, he might drown if he stuck his head in," Henrietta replied.

"I don't like to be wet...*chirrup*." Theodore hiccupped.

"Well, you don't like hiccups either," Rumples said.

The group led Theodore to the water trough. "Try a sip first. If that doesn't work, stick your head in," encouraged Rhody.

Theodore carefully lowered his beak into the water, tipped his head back, and let it slip down his gullet. "*Chirrup, chirrup, chirrup.*"

"Okay, put your whole head in," said Rumples with authority.

Theodore looked around anxiously. "Do I have to?"

"YES," they answered. "Just make sure you hold your breath first."

Theodore's tail feathers shook. He leaned over the trough and stuck his head into the water. Seconds later, he popped up. "I almost drowned in there! *Chirrup, chirrup.* And I still… *chirrup*…have the hiccups. I don't think I'll ever get rid of them."

Sly came by at just that moment. "Hey, wassup? Theodore, kid, you're all wet. And why are you hens all gathered round? What won't you ever get rid of?"

Rhody turned and gave Sly a firm peck. "Get out of here, you egg thief. Poor Theodore has the hiccups and we have to help him. Your help isn't needed."

"Did you forget my help saved Sissy at the pond? I can be helpful. But I don't have a cure for hiccups. Sorry, gotta go." Sly scurried off.

The guinea fowl gang noticed the gathering and wandered over.

"*Chirrup, chirrup, chirrup.*" Poor Theodore hiccupped his greeting.

"What is that noise coming out of your beak," said Puchie.

Numda and Egelli froze and looked around in terror. "Oh my, oh my. Is there some new beast in the barnyard? Shall we flee?"

"Theodore is making a strange noise," said Puchie.

"I have the…*chirrup, chirrup*…hiccups."

"What's that?"

"Is it contagious?"

"Oh dear, if I catch it, I could die."

"Hiccups, it sounds awful."

Each of the guinea fowl had a comment.

Officer Drake interrupted. "It's not fatal, and it's not contagious. If you can't help, go away and leave poor Theodore alone. He has enough problems without your foolishness."

"We don't know what hiccups are, so how do we know if we can help," Puchie said, his feathers fluffed in indignation.

"It's a spasm in your chest, like a burp, but it keeps happening and you can't stop it. We're trying to find a cure."

"OOH, OOH! I know, I know," said Gutterra. "I had that once. I flew up into a tall tree and then fell out. Cured them right away."

"Fall out of tree? That sounds painful," said Officer Drake.

"Hiccups...*chirrup, chirrup, chirrup*...are painful too. Do you think it'll work?" asked Theodore.

"It worked for me," Gutterra said.

Theodore took a running start, flew high into the tree next to the barnyard, and perched on a solid branch.

"Now, fall out," said Gutterra.

Theodore tipped forward, then back, then forward again. The ground looked so far away he couldn't get his feet to let go of the branch. Forward, then back, then forward. "I can't," he cried. "*Chirrup, chirrup.*"

"This just isn't going to work," said Sergeant Gander. "I don't think that was a very safe idea anyway."

"*Chirrup, chirrup.* Oh dear, they're getting worse."

Skeet skittered up the fence post. "Theodore, if you come with me to the farmhouse porch, I think I can cure your hiccups."

"I'll try anything."

Theodore flew from the branch, toward the farmhouse. On a table on the porch was an opened magazine. Theodore took one look, gasped, and his hiccups vanished.

"Wow, thanks, Skeet. *Gobble, gobble.* That did the trick. I got my gobble back."

Theodore returned to the barnyard. Rumples and all the chickens, Puchie and the rest of the guinea fowl, and the Geese Police gathered about in wonder. "What did Skeet do?" they all asked.

With a grin, Theodore gobbled, "He scared the stuffing out of me, right, Skeet?"

"Well…" Skeet nodded, "…I figured nothing would scare you more than a picture of a roasted Thanksgiving turkey."

The barnyard exploded in laughter as Theodore fluffed his tail feathers and gobbled his thanks to all his friends.

Chapter Seven

The Case of the Missing Kit

Mrs. Sylvi rushed into headquarters, frantic. "My baby, my precious kit. She's missing. Gone! Hurry, you have to find her. Please hurry."

The brown-and-beige cottontail hopped around on her strong hind legs, her long velvet ears twitching and crossing in agitation.

"Mrs. Sylvi, please sit down. Tell me what happened? Who's missing?" Officer Drake replied calmly.

"Peony. She wasn't in the burrow this morning. That girl is always taking off. She usually comes when I call her. I've searched high and low, up and down, over and under, and can't find her. Oh, I am so afraid something dreadful has happened. Please, Officer Drake, find my baby."

"Can you describe her to me?"

"She's a three-month-old cottontail rabbit. She looks just like me, only smaller. I don't know what gets into that girl. I would never worry my momma like she worries me."

"We'll put out an APB. I'm sure she will be found soon. You go home and we'll be in touch."

"Go home? I can't go home without my baby. Can I search with you?"

"It would be better if you stayed close to home. If she comes home, you can let us know, and we will know where to find you if we have any news. Please, Mrs. Sylvi, let us do our job."

Mrs. Sylvi hopped away reluctantly; her white cottontail twitched in distress.

Officer Drake honked for Sergeant Gander, and they left to post an all-points bulletin for the missing bunny. They told Skeet and Gar to be on the lookout. They asked the guinea fowl to report back on any sightings. They spread the word to the goats and even told the swan family at the pond. No one had seen the bunny.

Word spread fast. Marjorie Magpie sat on the fence post near the barnyard. Her white wing patches fluttered in the breeze. Her black beak opened and shut with her raucous calls. "Missing, did you hear? That bunny has no business worrying us like this. No consideration from kids these days. I declare. How thoughtless!"

"Marjorie, did it ever occur to you that Peony might be in trouble?" Gar hissed as he slithered by. "We have to help."

"Ungrateful bunny. That's what I have to say about it," she cawed as she flew off.

Marjorie Magpie flew into her large nest that rested in a tall oak tree in the middle of the meadow. She landed gracefully in the doorway and surveyed the area. She was always on the lookout for wonderful things to eat.

She knew every inch of the meadow and kept a wary eye out for things that didn't belong. Barely visible on the edge of the large bramblebush was a tiny bit of brown-and-grey fluff. Marjorie flew down from the tree and hopped quietly to the spiny bush.

"Peony? Is that you? Peony, what do you think you are doing, scaring your momma like that? Why she is near frantic with worry. What are you doing here, anyway?" Marjorie scolded.

Peony scooted back a bit into the brambles and waited for the bird to quit squawking.

"Oh, Ms. Magpie, I'm so glad to see you. I ran under here to get away from a hawk that was circling the meadow," Peony whispered.

"Well, what are you doing out in the meadow by yourself?"

"I followed a butterfly. He was flitting along so beautifully. I didn't pay attention to where I was. I found myself down at the pond. And when I tried to get home, I saw the hawk and hid in these bushes. And then I was so tired from running and being scared, I fell asleep. Momma must really be mad. Thank you for finding me. But, where am I?" Peony was breathless from all the telling, and she finally stopped and sat firmly on the ground. "Oh dear, am I lost again?"

Marjorie hopped back and forth in agitation. "Stay here and I'll get some help. Don't move until I return."

Marjorie flew over to the barnyard. "Officer Drake, Sergeant Gander, I found her; I found Peony. You have to come quickly."

"Marjorie, settle down. Where is she? Is she all right?" Sergeant Gander asked.

"She's in the meadow under the bramblebush. She fell asleep after being chased by a hawk. I told her to stay put until someone came for her."

"Officer Drake, follow Marjorie and escort Peony home. I'll go tell Mrs. Sylvi that Peony has been found."

Within minutes, Officer Drake was walking Peony toward her burrow. "Tsk, tsk" was all the officer had to say as Peony told him about her adventure.

Peony was scolded and nuzzled and scolded some more by her momma. "You naughty bunny. I should send you to bed without supper, but I am so glad to have you home safe and sound. Don't go running off like that ever again."

"Yes, Momma. I'm sorry I worried you. There was this lovely butterfly, you see."

Momma sighed. "Yes, Peony, I know."

The next day, Mrs. Sylvi went to the barnyard to thank the Geese Police for bringing her baby bunny back. The police were out on patrol. "I want to do something special to thank everyone who helped to spread the word," Mrs. Sylvi said. "I have the best grub ever for Marjorie, but I want to do something really special for the Geese Police."

"Let's have a party," said Henrietta. "We've all been helped by the Geese Police. We'll have a big thank-you party."

"Let's have a surprisssssse party," hissed Gar. "I love surprisssesss."

Chapter Eight

Horace

"Come quick. An intruder! He's digging over there." Frightened, Skeet stood on the rock, gasping for air.

"What are you talking about?" Sergeant Gander asked. "Take a breath; slow down; now tell me what's the problem?"

"There is a large animal in the woods. I saw him digging around the trees. He's making a real mess. He scared the bejeebers out of me. He had a big, flat, dirty nose, beady eyes, mottled skin, and a twisty tail," Skeet said as he made a twisting motion with his front foot. "He looked scary. Oh please, come quick."

Soon, the Geese Police were flying over the treetops, trying to spot the intruder. About halfway into the woods, under a large oak tree, they spotted something moving and dirt flying.

"Looks like we found the problem," Sergeant Gander said, watching the dirt fly.

"Excuse me, sir. Could you please state your name and where you've come from?" Officer Drake ordered in his most official voice.

A pink-and-gray snout covered with dirt and leaves rose from a hole in the ground next to a large oak. "I say, old chap. My name is Horace. I am a truffle pig."

"You've made quite a mess here and scared everyone. What are you doing?"

"Well, I woke up and found myself magically transported to this wonderful place. Now, I'm doing what I do." He stuck his head back into the hole.

"Magically transported? How is that even possible?" Officer Drake honked in disbelief.

"Well, I don't know what else to call it. I went to sleep and woke up here. I can't find my farmer, but I sure found lots of truffles," Horace said.

"What is a truffle? Why do you hunt them? What do you do with them?" Sergeant Gander asked.

"A truffle is a delicacy. I find them. The farmer collects them. I love the way they smell. See? I found some right here by this large tree."

The Geese Police peeked into the hole and saw some small, wrinkled nodes. "I don't smell anything. It just smells like damp dirt to me." Sergeant Gander turned and looked at Horace. "Well, we can't have you tearing up the woods."

Horace looked around. "Oh my, I really have been messy. You'll have to excuse me. Sometimes when I dig, I get carried away."

"Horace, if you keep digging around these trees, they could die, and then this beautiful area might disappear forever. You can't continue to cause such damage."

"How can I fix this?" The truffle pig paced back and forth in obvious agitation.

"Well, you can start by filling up the holes you dug. Then, join us in the barnyard, so we can properly introduce you to everyone. You frightened poor Skeet so bad he could barely breathe."

"Egad. I certainly didn't intend to do that. I am awfully sorry, old chap. I'll get right on it."

Horace started pushing the dirt back into the holes, tamping it down firmly with his snout. Every once in a while, he would start digging instead of filling. Sergeant Gander would have to remind him about the task at hand. "Focus, Horace. No more truffle hunting today."

"Right on. Thank you for reminding me." Horace continued to fill in the holes, but he also continued to lose focus.

When the woods were tidied up, the three went to the barnyard. There, they found Skeet retelling his scary adventure to anyone who would listen.

Skeet waved his arms around, and the animal got bigger with each telling. "You should have seen the beast. He was dirty, with teeth this…" holding his arms as far apart as he could, "…long."

Most of the barnyard animals wandered away after listening to his story for a second time. The guinea fowl, being the silliest animals in the area, listened to his tale over and over again.

"Oh my, oh my."

"The scary beast."

"Just as Skeet described. Those beady eyes!"

"Is he going to eat us?"

The guinea fowl ran in circles, in and out like a spiral puzzle, flapping their wings and complaining loudly.

Officer Drake watched the birds flutter and flap around. He looked over at Sergeant Gander and yelled, "Halt."

The kerfuffle ceased immediately. All eyes turned toward Officer Drake.

"I'm pleased to introduce you to Horace, a truffle pig. He's the one who has been messing up the woods. I would like to add that he has also put it back together. I'm sure he'd like to say a few words about himself."

"I say, what a fine-looking group of animals. Dear me, dear me. And here I am with my face a mess. I usually don't look like this, but, you see, there was this great oak with ever so many truffles hidden beneath the roots. Oh, it was a treasure trove."

"Ahem," Officer Drake cleared his throat. "Focus, Horace."

"Oh, yes indeed. Anyway, I am Horace. I have a superior nose that sniffs out truffles from under the ground. It's a most remarkable talent. They smell so sweet, you see. They just draw me like a bee to nectar. Truly remarkable."

"Horace!" Officer Drake yelled.

"Oh yes. Anyway, I came on a long journey just to be here. I hope we'll all be friends." He looked at the guinea fowl. "What a fine-looking group of guineas. I hope to get to know all of you. And who is this charming lady?" Horace winked at Henrietta, who fluffed her feathers.

"Oh goodness, we have a charmer in our midst," Rhody clucked. "We could do with a little culture around here. You have an accent. Where are you from?"

"I usually work in the forests around Dorset, England. This is my first time here. By the way, where is here? I'm so excited to meet all of you. Especially you charming ladies."

That sent up a flutter of cackles and chirps in the barnyard. Suddenly, Skeet skittered down the shade tree. "Well, you don't look so scary now. I'm Skeet. You gave me quite a fright in the woods."

"I say, old man, I am dreadfully sorry about that. When I look for truffles, I forget about everything else. It appears I might be around for a time. Is there somewhere I could clean up? I don't mind grubbing in the dirt while I'm working, but I really prefer to be clean."

Sly, the rat, ran over. "Come on, pal. I'll take you down to the pond."

Horace looked around at the barnyard family. "I'm so pleased to be here. Thank you."

He followed Sly across the yard to the pond. The swans looked on in interest. Sly said, "This is Horace. He's new here. I hope you'll be nice to him. He's a long way from home."

Buccinator replied, "We're always nice, except to rats."

"Hey, I helped Sissy, didn't I?"

"Yes, you did, and we are grateful. But I still don't like rats," Buccinator said.

"We're happy to meet you, Horace. Looks like you can use a bath. There is a nice shallow, private corner right around that bunch of reeds, near the rock." Molly pointed just as Sissy swam by.

"Mom, let me show him. Come on, Horace."

Grandfather Bullfrog was sitting on the rock when Horace reached the bathing site. "Excuse me, sir," Horace said. "My name is Horace. I was working today, and now I need a bath. I hope I am not disturbing you."

Grandfather Bullfrog puffed out his lovely yellow vest, snapped his tongue in and out as a mosquito flew by too close, smiled at Horace as he licked his lips, and said, "I'd be happy to share my pond with you."

Once nice and clean again, Horace walked back to the yard, feeling content. "Thank you all for your hospitality. I hope I can repay you someday."

"This is our barnyard family, Horace."

Officer Drake and Sergeant Gander were happy that Horace promised to clean up any mess he made in the woods, hunting for truffles. They were also pleased with his acceptance in the barnyard.

"Well, it looks like another crisis averted. The Geese Police serve and protect," Sergeant Gander said, and they both flew over the barnyard.

Chapter Nine

Gabby

Officer Drake heard sobbing. He searched the bushes behind the barn; there he found Gabby in a puddle of tears. "Gabby, are you hurt? What's wrong? Shall I call for help?"

"Oh, Officer Drake, you weren't supposed to see me like this. I look a mess. I'm sorry. It's just that everyone hates me," with a hiccup, she sobbed as she spoke.

Officer Drake spoke with a calm, soothing tone, "I'm sure that's not true. You are a perfectly normal-looking alpaca with your silky-soft coat. Although I really don't know you very well, you seem quite nice."

Gabby looked up and sniffed.

"Why would you think that everyone hates you? I don't hate you, and I'm someone." He tried not to set her off again.

"Well, it all started this morning when I was talking to the goats and Horace in the pasture. Marjorie Magpie flew over to listen to the conversation. I happened to mention Horace having a dirty face. He started an argument. Marjorie repeated everything I said," she explained.

"That doesn't seem so bad to me. Did Horace have a dirty face? Was he embarrassed?" Officer Drake asked.

"Yes to both. But that wasn't the problem. You see, when I'm mad, I have this bad habit. I spit. I don't mean to. Not really. Sometimes I can't help myself. Everyone thought it was disgusting. Poor Horace was in shock. Marjorie couldn't wait to spread the news. I am so ashamed. Nobody will ever like me again."

"These problems seem to be above my pay grade. Let's go find Sergeant Gander. He may have a solution." Officer Drake waddled towards HQ, but Gabby didn't follow. She stayed behind the bushes.

"I can't be seen looking like this. Everyone will make fun of me. Oh, I'm so embarrassed. I'll just stay here for the rest of my life." Gabby started crying again.

"I don't think that is a very practical solution. As long as you are with me, you'll be fine." Officer Drake stood as tall as he could. "I'll protect you."

Gabby came out of hiding. Her ears drooped; her eyes were red; her nose was a bit drippy. She looked a mess.

Officer Drake reassured her, "See, it's going to be fine."

Before they reached HQ, they heard voices coming from the guinea fowl. "Gabby, Gabby, spits and drools. Spit on Horace; she's a fool."

Gabby ran and hid behind a big tree. "See, they hate me." She cried large tears, almost flooding the area.

Officer Drake strode over to the guinea flock. "Stop that right now. Don't you know how mean you're being?"

"We're not mean. We didn't spit on anyone. It was that tall, fuzzy animal hiding behind the tree."

"You didn't spit on anyone, but teasing her is mean. Here's the facts. She's an alpaca; they spit when they are angry. It's part of their nature. Just like your nature is to be foolish. We live here together; we need to be kind and considerate of each other."

Losing interest in Officer Drake, one of the guinea fowl found some seeds in the far corner of the pen and yelled, "Food." All the fowl took off across the yard lickety-split. They argued and shoved in an attempt to get to the food first.

"Well, so much for my lecture. Come along, Gabby, we were on our way to HQ. Maybe we'll be lucky and find Judge Hoot there too. He always has some wise words."

Upon arriving at headquarters, Officer Drake and Gabby discovered a large crowd of animals out front.

"There she is."

"She spit."

"That is so rude."

"We don't want her in our barnyard."

All the voices talked at once. Sergeant Gander just stood and quietly waited for the fuss to die down a bit.

"Officer Drake, I see you found our little problem." He smiled and winked at Gabby, who openly sobbed again.

"I'm so sorry," she hiccupped through the tears. "I didn't mean to cause such a problem."

Tired of the commotion, he blew his whistle for silence. "Horace, was your face dirty?"

"Yes sir, I'd been hunting for truffles and hadn't washed up yet. Truffle hunting is what I do."

"Fine. Marjorie Magpie, did you fly around gossiping about what happened?"

"Of course, it's what I do. I can't change that," Marjorie said.

"I'm not bringing the foolish guinea fowl into the discussion. That would get us nowhere. Is there anyone here who can change who they are and what they do?" Sergeant Gander asked.

"Well, alpacas spit. It's what they do. They aren't being mean, or rude, or nasty. They don't hate you when they spit. It's part of their nature. We probably need to be more tolerant of each other's foibles. It's the best way I know to get along," Sergeant Gander stated. "Do you think you can do that?"

Heads bobbed up and down throughout the barnyard. "Now, some apologies are in order. Just because you can't help it, doesn't mean you shouldn't apologize for hurting someone. Gabby, you first."

"I'm sorry I spit. I promise I'll try not to do it again, but if it happens, I hope you will forgive me," Gabby said.

"Marjorie, you are next." Sergeant Gander looked pointedly at the bird and waited for an argument.

Marjorie just lowered her head and said, "Sorry. I promise not to spread gossip, but if I do, I hope you'll forgive me."

Horace came next. "When I hunt for truffles, my nose gets dirty. I guess I shouldn't be so touchy about an innocent comment. I'm sorry I started an argument. I'll try not to be offended, but if it happens again, I hope you'll forgive me."

"There now, do you think we can all get along?" Officer Drake asked.

Just then, Judge Hoot appeared in the doorway. "This was a wonderful solution to the problem. But I have one more thing to add. Here, Gabby. Maybe this will help you with the spitting problem. Look, it matches your silky coat."

He handed her an attractive mask to wear when she was out talking and walking, and liable to get into an argument.

Gabby tried it on. Everyone commented on how wonderful it looked on her. Gabby sashayed around the barnyard, showing off her new mask.

Chapter Ten

Ellie

"I won't come out. Mom, please don't make me. I'm so embarrassed. How could you let them do this to me?" Ellie sobbed. "I'm naked," she whispered through her tears.

"You are not naked. You were sheared. They took all the extra wool off so you would be more comfortable in the coming summer months. Ellie, it is just fine. And you look terrific."

"Mom, I look awful. I'm just going to stay here for the rest of my life. I will never go out with the herd again. I can't be seen in the meadow like this. All my friends will laugh at me. You just don't understand." Ellie stomped off on her dainty hooves, sniffing her misery.

"Honestly, Lucille. I don't know what I'm going to do with her. These teenage years can be really trying. She's hiding in the barn because she thinks she's naked. They gave her a wonderful shear job. She looks terrific. And she thinks she's naked. Kids nowadays. Why, when I was her age, we didn't have hysterics because of shearing time. We felt so fresh and pretty. And the boys thought we were so pretty. Oh, to be young again."

"Dotty, you are so bad." She laughed. Her friend was a bit of a flirt, and motherhood hadn't changed her. "But what are you going to do about Ellie?"

"I'm hoping the problem will resolve itself. A few days of isolation will probably drive her out and back to the herd. Lambs usually get lonely very quickly. I think I'll just ignore the drama and let her sulk." Dotty saw a nice, juicy clump of grass and moved quickly to chew it down.

"These kinds of issues usually don't go away. They just get worse," Lucille said as she walked away.

Ellie wandered the barn, hiding behind a wagon and then a stack of tools. She finally made her way to the bales of hay without anyone seeing her. "I can't believe it. Mom just doesn't understand." Ellie sniffed and pouted, feeling very sorry for herself. She was hungry too. All the nice green grass was in the pasture. "I can't go there. I look so awful." And she cried again.

Horace, taking a break from his truffle hunting, was hanging around the barnyard. "I say there, missy, why are you crying in the barn. It is a beautiful spring day. I, myself, just came in for some shade. Are you hiding?"

"Shhh. I can't let anyone see me. I look terrible. I am so humiliated. They took my lovely coat off today. Why, I am positively naked," Ellie sobbed.

"Come, come now. It can't be that bad. Let me have a look. I'll be honest about the whole thing, and no one will ever have to know," Horace replied.

Ellie edged out from behind the hay bales. "Look what they did to me."

"Oh my. Well, you certainly look skinny. And your coat is very short. I suppose it will grow again. But then, I'm no judge of that. I don't think you look so bad." Horace tried to be supportive.

"So bad. Oh no," Ellie wailed more loudly. "I'm ruined. I'm going to stay in here for the rest of my life."

Horace sighed and left. He was sorry he had caused more anguish. He met Officer Drake on his way to the pond.

"Hi, Horace. What's up?"

"Hello, Officer. I thought I'd cool off in the wet dirt by the pond. It is a hot day for early spring. I found Ellie crying in the barn. She is all upset over her shearing. I don't think I helped with my comments. There is surely a lot of excitement in this barnyard." Horace continued on his way to the pond.

Officer Drake sighed. *I better go check on Ellie,* he thought. *Let's see if I can help her feel better.*

"Ellie? Ellie, are you in here? It's Officer Drake. Can you come out so I can talk with you?"

Officer Drake heard a scratching noise from behind the bales of hay. Then a quiet sneeze. "Ellie, come on, we need to talk. You can't stay here forever. Aren't you getting hungry?"

"Yes. I'm starving. And my mother doesn't care. Nobody cares. I could die and nobody would care." Ellie sniffed. "And just look at me. I look hideous. And Mom let them do it. I hate her."

"Okay, I know. It's awful, and the world is treating you unfairly. But don't you think maybe we can find a different way to solve this besides hiding in the barn and being hungry? Let's see, what can we use?"

Ellie's eyes got big. "You mean you're going to help me?"

"Of course. That's what we do." He was pleased to see that she was coming out of hiding.

"Oh, Officer Drake, you are the best." Ellie went running toward him.

"Well, let me think of something first. Then see how you feel about it." He smiled.

Officer Drake searched the barn, and finally in the upper loft under a small saddle was an old saddle blanket. "Aha, I think we can solve your problem."

Officer Drake placed the blanket over Ellie's back. "Now, be very careful not to bounce it off. You have to walk with a dignified air, but this will hide the shearing job. If you can keep it on for a week or two, your fleece will grow out, and you'll have your beautiful coat back. Until then, you will have a very stylish robe. Why, you'll be the envy of all your friends."

"Officer Drake, I don't know how to thank you. You are so wonderful. This makes me feel so much better." Ellie leaped for joy, and the blanket started to slip off. "Oh my, I guess I can't do that."

"Come on, I'll walk you to the pasture." Officer Drake motioned to the door.

Ellie walked very slowly to the pasture, even though she was really eager to run. She was hungry and was looking forward to visiting with her friends. She wanted to show off her blanket.

And there were her friends. They were jumping, running, playing, and eating. And they had all been sheared.

Ellie took off toward them, dropping her blanket in the process.

Officer Drake looked on in amusement. *Another problem solved*, he thought. *All in a day's work.*

Chapter Eleven

Baxter

"What happened here? My burrow! Part of my burrow is destroyed. I had my home just perfect, and now look at it. *Frumblemush!* I better not run into that bully who ruins homes. He will definitely get a piece of my mind." Baxter paced back and forth, occasionally sticking his head up through the entrance to check and see if anyone else was around.

Baxter heard a rustling noise. "Who's there? Come out, you scoundrel."

"I say, old man. I'm terribly sorry. Was this your home? It looks terribly comfortable. Let me tidy it up," Horace said.

"Who are you, and why have you broken into my house?"

"I'm Horace. I am a truffle pig. And you are?"

Pulling his hefty body to full height out of the hole, he said, "I am Baxter. I am a groundhog and a shadow keeper. I would really appreciate it if you didn't hunt for truffles under my tree. What are truffles, anyway?"

"What is a shadow keeper? I've never heard of that. How does one keep shadows?" Horace quizzed.

"I have a little shadow that goes everywhere with me, and what can be the use of him is more than I can see," Baxter replied.

"Whatever do you mean, old chap? I'm afraid I understand very little of what you are saying."

"Well, why not? I speak clearly. You're the one who broke into my house, and you want me to explain myself to you? Who do you think you are?" Baxter paced in agitation.

"Sorry, old pal. I promise to avoid your tree from now on. I certainly did not intend to cause a problem. But I really am intrigued with shadow keeping. Please tell me more."

"Well, I suppose I can fix my home back up. And if you promise not to do more damage, I won't report you to the

Geese Police. Help me fix my home, and I'll try to explain about shadows."

Horace started smoothing out the dirt at the tip of the hole. Baxter crawled back inside to shore up the ceiling of his home. Between the two of them, they had it done in no time at all.

"Thanks for the help. You did a good job of putting things back together, but then it was you that tore it up."

"You're welcome. Now, do I get to find out about shadows?" Horace asked.

"My shadow is short; my shadow is tall. My shadow will hide, so he's not there at all. He'll never come play in the dark of the moon, and he'll stick to my heel when the sun reaches noon," Baxter recited as he looked very pensive.

"Why are you speaking so weird? What does this have to do with shadow keeping?"

Baxter humphed. "I am a poet. I have explained what shadows do. Obviously, I am wasting my talent trying to explain." Baxter humphed again and dove into his hole.

"Oh my, I'm terribly afraid I have insulted my new friend. I best go talk to the Geese Police."

Officer Drake was watching the swans in the pond. He loved the graceful way they glided across the surface. The cygnets were exploring, curious about every movement of the reeds.

"Officer Drake, look what I can do." Sissy dove under the water, wiggle-waggled her webbed feet in the air, did an underwater pirouette, and popped back up to the surface.

"You've become such a good swimmer, Sissy. Just be careful with your acrobatics. We don't want you getting tangled up in something again," Drake said.

"Yea, that was scary. But I know better now. I'm careful. Want me to show you more?"

"Thanks, but no, Sissy. I think I just want to sit here and be quiet for a bit. It's been a long week." He enjoyed the relaxed feel of the breeze blowing over the water.

Horace approached the pond with reluctance. He hated to disturb the peaceful scene. "Ahem, excuse me, Officer, may I speak with you?"

"Aw, Horace. What can I do for you?"

"Well, sir, I met this interesting animal in the woods today. I'm afraid I accidentally broke into his home. He scolded me quite roundly. I helped him repair the damage, so we're fine there."

Officer Drake sighed and looked intensely at Horace. "Why do I feel that isn't the end of the story?"

"Officer, his name was Baxter, and he said he is a shadow keeper. He spouted poetry, but wouldn't tell me what a shadow keeper is. I'm afraid I insulted him with my questions. I just want to understand," Horace said quietly.

"So you met our groundhog! He is one colorful character. Baxter comes from a long line of groundhogs who help decide when spring comes. They keep their shadow in their home all winter long; then just before spring, they peek out of the hole. If their shadow comes with them, we will have six more weeks of winter; if the shadow stays in bed, it will be an early spring."

"I see. A shadow keeper. But why all the rhyme?" Horace asked.

"He likes poetry and fancies himself a poet. He may quote it or make it up. He's just fun to listen to. I'm glad you met him. I'm sure you'll be great friends."

Horace sighed. "I'm not so sure. He was awfully mad at me when I left. Is there something I can do to make it up to him?"

"As I said, he loves poetry. Give him a poem as an apology. That will put him in a good mood."

"Thanks, Officer. That's exactly what I'll do." Horace ran off, trying to devise a poem in his head.

He started off with "I'm sorry," but couldn't find anything to rhyme with sorry. He thought of other ways to say sorry, like "apologize." Still no luck with rhymes. "This is harder than it looks. And to think he just made up something right there in front of me. Wow, he really is good."

He thought and he thought all night long. By morning, he had an idea. He hurried to Baxter's tree and spoke softly down the hole. He didn't want to startle his friend by hollering. "Baxter, may I talk to you for a minute?"

Baxter peeped out of the hole, wiping his sleepy eyes. "It's early; what do you want?"

"I need help, and since you write such excellent poetry, I was hoping you could help me," Horace pleaded.

Baxter puffed up with the praise. "I'll be glad to help. Why do you need a poem?"

"I thought it might be the perfect way to apologize for a mistake I made. I tried to do it myself, but I couldn't figure out how to rhyme with 'sorry.' I thought I'd ask an expert."

Baxter got very thoughtful. "Many words are hard to rhyme. I find a word that is easy and use it instead. Let's see if I can help:

Horace is sorry for his mistake.

If he knew how, he'd bake you a cake.

He promises to try and not do it again.

If he does, you can stick him with a pin."

Horace laughed. "Well, it wasn't exactly what I had in mind, but I think it covers the ground. You just provided me with the perfect apology to you. Thank you."

Baxter laughed. "See what happens when you ask an expert. Me and my shadow both thank you."

Chapter Twelve

The Wild-Goose Chase

"Oh no! They are back already," Henrietta clucked. "I don't know what else to do."

"Well, I tried. I sent them out to the meadow to break up a fight," Skeet said. "Marjorie's voice almost started a riot with the meadowlark choir."

"I sent them down to the pond," Grandfather Bullfrog croaked. "It didn't take them long to figure out the snake was only a reed waving in the current."

"We don't have enough time to get anything done, and I've run out of excuses," complained Mrs. Sylvi. "How will we ever get this party together?" Her whiskers twitched excitedly.

Judge Hoot perched on a fence post and said, "Don't worry! I can keep them busy all afternoon. Send them to my chambers."

Sergeant Gander looked about. "Have you noticed lots of strange calls, and none of them amount to anything at all."

"Yes, very strange," said Officer Drake.

"Judge Hoot wants to see both of you at HQ," said Sly as he skittered by.

"What about?" Officer Drake asked.

"I don't know. Bad enough he makes me the messenger boy," Sly said as he darted under the gate.

The geese waddled towards Judge Hoot's chambers.

"Good afternoon, gentlemen," Judge Hoot said and pointed to a stack of papers. "I found some incomplete reports. I need these finished right away."

Sergeant Gander looked in dismay at the stack of paperwork, and then saw Officer Drake trying to sidle out of the office. "Oh no, you don't," Gander said. "Judge Hoot called us both here." With a sigh, they resigned themselves to spending the afternoon buried in reports.

Out in the barnyard, preparations were finally in full swing. The hens gathered food. The guinea fowl flew up and down, over and around all the branches, hanging decoration. Sly decorated the corncrib, and Gar kept a sharp eye out for the return of the Geese Police. Beetal, Myo, and the rest of goats brought grass and twigs for soft cushions.

Grandfather Bullfrog practiced his introduction. He was going to be the emcee. Skeet darted back and forth, relaying orders and instructions to everyone who had questions.

Marlo waddled into the middle of the excitement. "What can I do?" he asked. "I didn't come all this way just to stand around," he said crustily.

"Make sure there is enough seating for everyone," clucked Rhody.

Rumples, Andy, and Henrietta hurried by with bowls of corn and oats.

Marlo moved closer to the arena where the event was going to take place. "Who's all coming and how many are there?" he asked.

"Let'ssss sssee," Gar hissed. "Judge Hoot, who isss keeping our guestsss of honor busssy today. Ssskeet and Sssly. The four henss, six goatss, including Beetal and Myo, all the guinea fowl, Theodore, the ssswan family, Marjorie Magpie, Mrs. Sssylvi, Peony and her sssistersss, Grandfather Bullfrog, you, and me."

"Goodness, this will be some party," Marlo said, surprised at the number.

"Well, the Geessse Police helped almost everyone I mentioned," Gar replied.

Buccinator, Molly, Sissy, and the other cygnets arrived and helped with the final preparations.

Grandfather Bullfrog hopped up on the stage. He looked very elegant in his yellow, spotted waistcoat. *"Croak, croak, testing, croak,"* he said into the sound system.

"Looks like everything is working just fine. Now, where are the honorees?" Sly asked.

"I'm keeping them busy as long as needed," Judge Hoot said from atop his branch. "Where's the entertainment?"

Just then, the meadowlarks arrived and got into formation on the stage behind Grandfather Bullfrog. Everyone was dressed in their finest. Theodore's tail feathers spread out in full color. The swans' feathers had a wonderful sheen. Even the guinea fowl were neat and tidy. Myo arrived with Beetal and said, "Oh, this is so exciting. I hope I don't faint. I don't want to miss a minute."

Marjorie Magpie flew to the stage area. "Thank you so much for letting me conduct the concert. I promise I won't sing a note. Oh my, this is just too fun," she cawed to the meadowlarks.

Soon, everyone was in place. Judge Hoot returned to his office and said excitedly, "Officer Drake, Sergeant Gander, hurry. You're needed in the barnyard. All the rest of this can wait."

As the Geese Police landed in the yard, a roar went up from the gathering. *Clucks, quacks, gobbles,* and *cheeps* created quite a noise.

"Surprise!" they all yelled.

Grandfather Bullfrog introduced the meadowlark choir and Maestra Marjorie Magpie. After three thrilling songs, Judge Hoot took the stage.

"Everyone has gathered here today," he said in his most important-sounding voice, "to honor and pay our respects to our very own Geese Police." He cleared his throat to continue, but the cheers drowned him out.

The Geese Police puffed with pride as they took the stage to receive their medals. Judge Hoot drew a scroll from his robe that read, "In honor of your dedicated service to all the members of the barnyard, we at Harrow's Farm proclaim this to be Geese Police Day."

Officer Drake smiled. "I knew something suspicious was going on."

Sergeant Gander bowed his long neck and honked a quiet "thank you" while trying to wipe away a tear. Then they went around and greeted all those who had gathered to honor them.

Peony hopped to the stage and rubbed up against them. "My heroes," she said shyly.

Marjorie Magpie flew over and raucously cawed, "Hey, Peony, I'm the one who found you. Don't I get a hug too?"

"As long as you promise not to sing," Peony replied with a smile.

The laughter was heard across the meadow.

"Officer Drake, Sergeant Gander, I saw a weasel on the edge of the farm. He was slinking along, all furry and brown."

"Which way, Numda?" Sergeant Gander asked. After getting the directions he said, "We're on our way to protect and serve."

As they flew across the barnyard, Officer Drake replied, "Yup. Geese Police on patrol."

Glossary of Terms

A

Andy – Andalusian chickens. Can run very fast. An active breed, usually black and grey, with white to chalky-white, large to extra-large eggs.

APB – all-points bulletin.

B

Beetal – breed from Punjab region of India and Pakistan. Known as Amritsari goat.

Buccinator – Cygnus Buccinator or trumpeter swan.

Bullfrog – amphibian. Olive-green back and sides, with whitish belly spotted with yellow or grey. Male frog's call is similar to the roar of a bull. The sound is where it gets its name.

Burrow – hole or tunnel in the ground for habitat or refuge.

C

Cygnet – young or baby swan.

Chickens – many different colors and breeds, and lay colorful eggs ranging from white to green, brown to cream.

Cottontail rabbits – common rodent with a stub tail that has white undersides. Rarely found outside on windy days as it interferes with their hearing. Hearing an oncoming predator is their primary defense mechanism.

Crested guinea fowl – blackish plumage with white spots. Distinctive black crest on top of its head.

D

Drake – male duck or goose.

E

Edourdi – crested guinea fowl.

Egelli – black guinea fowl with an unfeathered head and upper neck. Males have one to three spurs.

Emcee – master of ceremonies.

G

Gander – male goose.

Garter snake – garden snake. Heterothermic, meaning it basks in the sun to get warm. May coil and strike but usually hides. Carnivorous, eats slugs, earthworms, and small amphibians, among other things. Food is swallowed whole.

Guinea fowl – birds from the family Numididae. Come in a variety of colors. Are not solitary fowl, tend to move together in a swarm.

Guttera – plumed guinea fowl.

H

Helmeted guinea fowl – large round body with a small head. Head is unfeathered, with a large, bony knob and blue skin patches.

Henrietta – Sussex breed. Speckled red, lays cream-colored eggs.

HQ – police headquarters.

K

Keets – young guinea fowl.

M

Maestra – Conductor of music.

Magpie – flashy relative of jays and crows.

Magpie nest – domed, usually thirty inches high and twenty inches wide, made of sticks, mud, and grass.

Mrs. Sylvi – genus Sylvilagus.

Muskrat – semi-aquatic rodent. Omnivorous, eats cattails and yellow water lilies. Can stay underwater twelve to seventeen minutes. Nests are called push-ups and can be found in lakes, ponds, and canals. Winter severity of weather is said to be predicted by the size of the lodge.

Myo – myotonic goat. Freezes when panicked. Smaller in size than regular goats.

N

Numda – helmeted guinea fowl.

P

Poison oak – dense shrub. Grows in open sunlight. Member of the Sumac family and causes itching and rashes to humans. Grows below 5,000 feet.

Puchie – crested guinea fowl.

R

Rhody – Rhode Island Red. Popular breed, good egg layer, lays brown eggs.

Rumples – Araucana or rumpless chicken. Has ear tufts and lays blue eggs.

S

Swans – mate for life. One of the heaviest birds capable of flight. Five to six feet long and fifteen to thirty pounds.

W

Wattle – fleshy caruncle hanging from various parts of birds or mammals.

Made in United States
North Haven, CT
25 September 2022